SNAKES
ON THE
JOB

KATHRYN DENNIS

Feiwel and Friends
New York

For little builders everywhere

A Feiwel and Friends Book
An imprint of Macmillan Publishing Group, LLC
120 Broadway, New York, NY 10271

Snakes on the Job. Copyright © 2020 by Kathryn Dennis. All rights reserved.
Printed in China by RR Donnelley Asia Printing Solutions Ltd.,
Dongguan City, Guangdong Province.

Our books may be purchased in bulk for promotional, educational, or business use.
Please contact your local bookseller or the Macmillan Corporate and Premium Sales Department
at (800) 221-7945 ext. 5442 or by email at MacmillanSpecialMarkets@macmillan.com.

Library of Congress Cataloging-in-Publication Data

Names: Dennis, Kathryn, author, illustrator.
Title: Snakes on the job / Kathryn Dennis.
Description: First edition. | New York : Feiwel and Friends, 2020. | Summary:
Illustrations and easy-to-read text follow a crew of snakes as they slide
into trucks, operate a crane, and line up at the lunch truck, working
together to reach their goal.
Identifiers: LCCN 2019018180 | ISBN 978-1-250-21400-3 (hardcover)
Subjects: | CYAC: Snakes—Fiction. | Construction equipment—Fiction. |
Building—Fiction.
Classification: LCC PZ7.D42778 Sr 2020 | DDC [E]—dc23
LC record available at https://lccn.loc.gov/2019018180

Book design by Sophie Erb
Feiwel and Friends logo designed by Filomena Tuosto
First edition, 2020

The artwork in this book was created digitally.

1 3 5 7 9 10 8 6 4 2

mackids.com

Off to work the snakes will go.

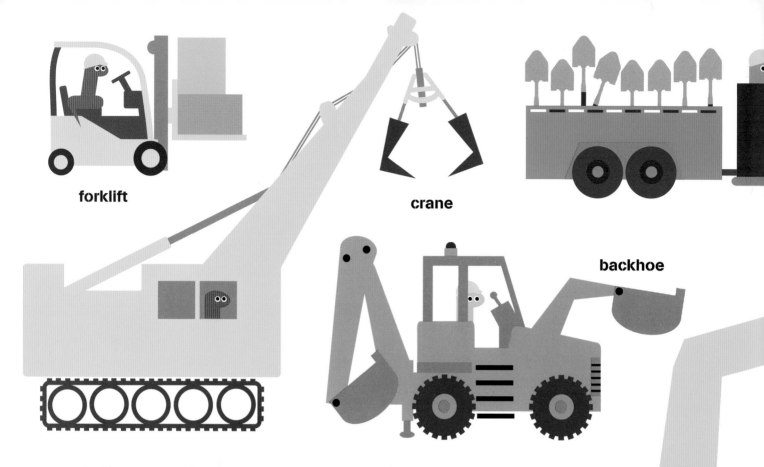

forklift

crane

backhoe

They slide into trucks
and roll out slow.

digger/excavator

PLAYTIME

delivery truck

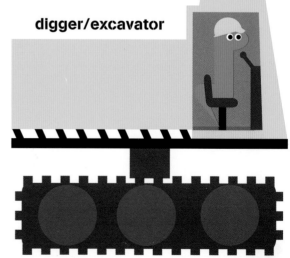

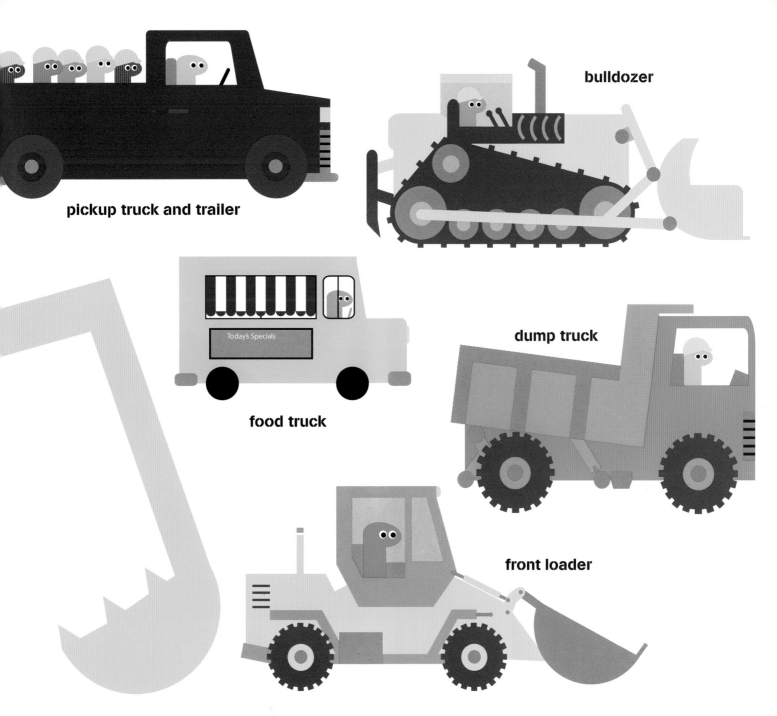

pickup truck and trailer

bulldozer

food truck

Today's Specials

dump truck

front loader

Hisssssssssssssh goes the sound of the brakes.

A digger clears the way

as a bulldozer shoves the dirt to one side.

Dump trucks are piled high.

Hisssssssssssssh goes the sound of the brakes.

PLAYTIME

A row of delivery trucks

keeps snakes moving at a steady pace.

A crane lifts large objects and swings them into place.

Hisssssssssh goes the sound of the brakes.

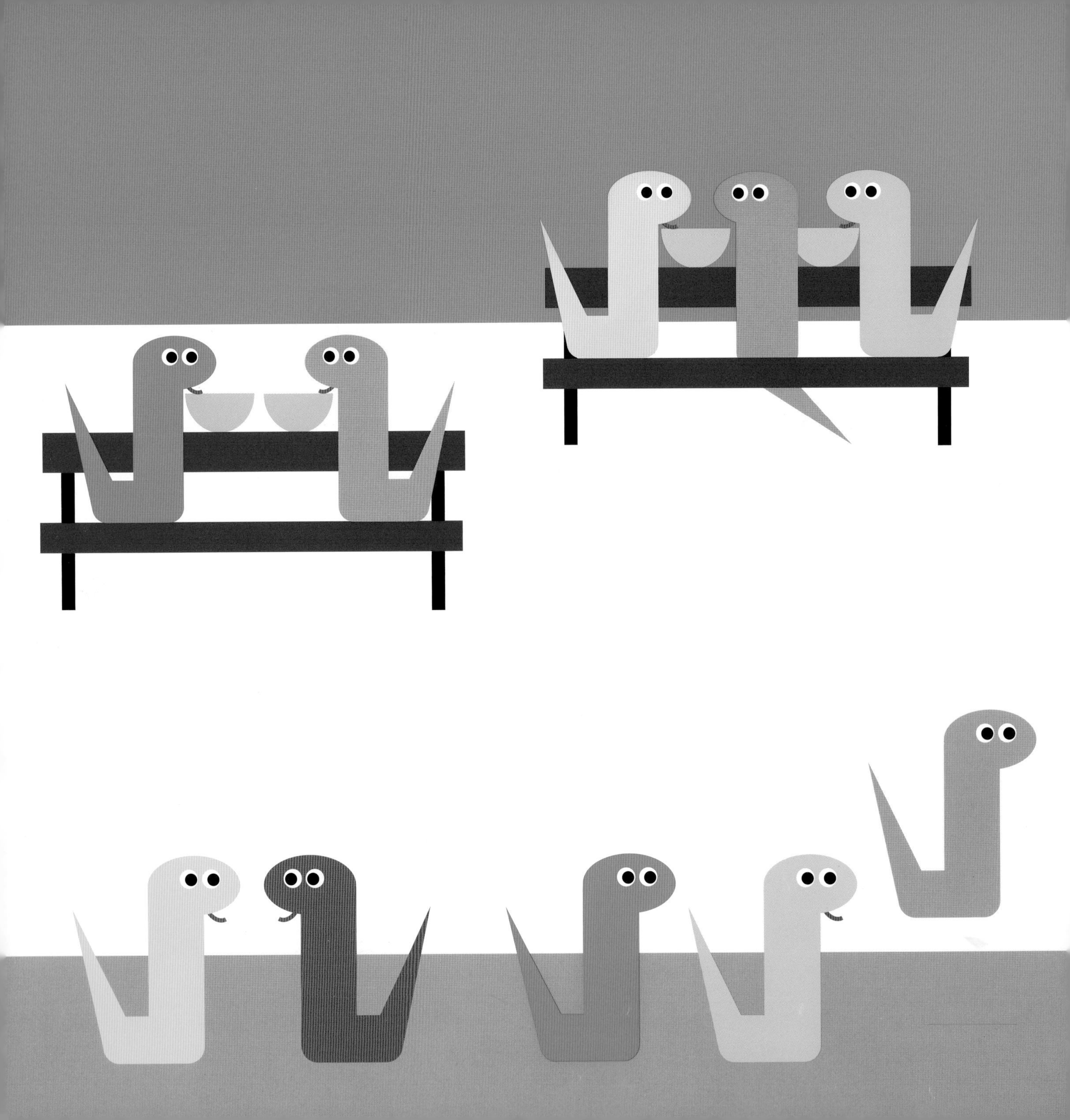

A food truck arrives and the
snakes line up for lunch.

Then it's back to work.

There's a time crunch.

A front loader rumbles in. Holes are dug and flowers fill wheelbarrows.

Hissssssssssssssh goes the sound of the brakes.

It takes three snakes to roll

a giant wheel into place.

Snakes work together to reach their goal.

A backhoe is needed to put in posts.
The project is coming to a close.

Hisssssssssssssh goes the sound of the brakes.

It's time to see what the snakes have built.

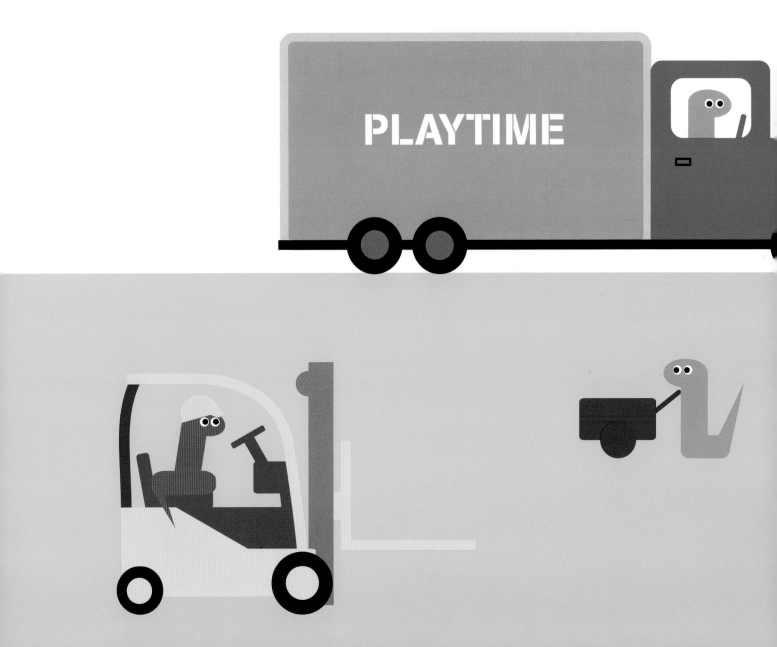

Hissssssssssh go the happy snakes.

Hamsters ask if they can play.
What will the snakes say?

WELCOME!

Yessssssssssh.